Lumber Camp Library

NATALIE KINSEY-WARNOCK

illustrated by James Bernardin

HarperTrophy®
An Imprint of HarperCollins*Publishers*

Lumber Camp Library
Text copyright © 2002 by Natalie Kinsey-Warnock
Illustrations copyright © 2002 by James Bernardin

Library of Congress Cataloging-in-Publication Data
Kinsey-Warnock, Natalie.
Lumber camp library / by Natalie Kinsey-Warnock ; illustrated by
James Bernardin.
p. cm.
Summary: Ruby wants to be a teacher, but after her father's death in a
logging accident she must quit school to care for her ten brothers and
sisters, until a chance meeting with a lonely old blind woman transforms
her life.
ISBN 0-06-029321-7 — ISBN 0-06-029322-5 (lib. bdg.)
ISBN 0-06-444292-6 (pbk.)
[1. Single-parent families—Fiction. 2. Books and reading—Fiction.
3. Loggers—Fiction. 4. Literacy—Fiction. 5. Teaching—Fiction. 6.
Blind—Fiction. 7. Physically handicapped—Fiction.] I. Bernardin,
James, ill. II. Title.
PZ7.K6293 Lu 2002   2001039684
[Fic]—dc21   CIP
                                                           AC

Typography by Larissa Lawrynenko

First Harper Trophy edition, 2003
Visit us on the World Wide Web!
www.harperchildrens.com

For Desi

Lumber Camp
Library

1

RUBY WAS BORN in 1912 in a lumber camp in the northern hills of Vermont. It was a bitter January night with drifts as high as the roof.

Pa hitched up one of the workhorses and drove six miles through the snow to fetch the doctor, but Ruby got there before the doctor did.

Pa cradled the new baby in his rough hands that cut timber all day long.

"My jewel," he said, "my little jewel," and named the baby Ruby.

As Ruby grew, she followed Pa everywhere. Pa seemed as much a part of the woods as the trees themselves. He taught her the names of the birds and the trees. She learned the tracks of bobcat and fox. Pa showed her where the wild ginger and lady slippers grew. Ma teased her about being Pa's little shadow, but Ruby didn't mind. She liked being Pa's shadow. Pa was her sun and moon and the stars in between, and anything he was doing, why, that was what she wanted to be doing, too.

In the years to follow, ten more sisters and brothers were born—Lillian, Marvin, Irene, Mabel, Albert, June, Lewis, Margaret, and the twins, Wilson and Ben. Pa loved them all, but it was Ruby he called his little jewel to the end of his days.

All winter long, Pa and the other lumberjacks cut down trees and piled the logs beside the river. In the spring, when the ice went out and the water was high, the logs were floated down the river to sawmills far away. It was Pa's job to make sure logs didn't get caught on rocks or bends in the river. If they did, the logs would pile up into a terrible jam. Pa then had to try to untangle that jumble of logs. Sometimes it took dynamite to blow a jam apart.

Some loggers died under falling trees or behind teams of horses, but it was the river that was the hardest and most dangerous place to work. The men worked all day, waist deep in icy water, lifting logs off sandbars and prying logjams apart. But it was the place Pa loved best. And he shone in riding the logs down the river.

All rivermen could stand on a log and ride it down through rapids, but Pa rode logs the way most men sit a chair. He made riding logs through churning water look like the easiest thing in the world. Pa could do handstands and somersaults on the log, and he could lie down on it while it went over the falls. That log would be bucking like a horse, and Pa would lie there with his eyes closed as if he were taking a nap. Ruby never tired of watching him.

Like other rivermen, Pa wore boots with sharp metal spikes in the soles to help him ride the logs. One day Pa showed Ruby a pair of old rotting boots hung on a tree beside the river.

"These were Jake Bowman's," Pa said. "Whenever a riverman drowns, it's custom to hang his spiked boots on a tree to mark the spot. It's our way of paying tribute."

A gray jay squawked from a nearby tree, and Pa jumped. It wasn't like Pa to be startled.

"What's the matter, Pa?" Ruby asked.

"Most lumberjacks are a superstitious lot," Pa said. "They call those jays 'moosebirds' and believe them to be the souls of dead lumberjacks. It's said you must never harm a moosebird or terrible things will happen to you."

Ruby watched the jay flit off through the trees.

"Do you believe that, Pa?" she asked. "Do you think that jay was Jake Bowman?"

"Well," Pa said slowly, "I'm not sure I believe that, but I let 'em be. You know, those birds are pests in camp. They'll steal bacon right out of the frying pan and carry off anything that catches their fancy, especially something bright and shiny. I had one steal a button right off my coat once, but I've never hurt one. I like 'em. You won't see 'em in towns; they're a bird of lonely places, a creature of the north woods." Pa grinned.

"Kinda like me," he said.

2

BY THE TIME RUBY was ten, Pa had taught her how to use an ax and a peavey, and how to drive horses. In camp she practiced balancing on logs, forward and backward and even with her eyes closed, and dreamed about being a lumberjack just like Pa. But Ma had other plans.

"It's well past time you went to school, Ruby," Ma said. "I hope you'll teach school someday. You know I was a teacher before I met your pa."

Ruby trembled. The thought of going into town made her mouth feel as dry as cornmeal. Pa seemed to read her thoughts.

"Once you learn to read, you can bring your books home and read to me. Your ma's so busy with all you kids, she doesn't have much time to read out loud, and you know I love a good story."

Pa knew so many things that sometimes Ruby forgot he couldn't read. He'd started working in the woods when he was eight, to help support a large family of brothers and sisters.

"Why do I have to go to school, Pa?" Ruby asked. "You didn't."

Pa kissed the top of her head.

"Because I want my children to be smarter than I am," he said.

Ruby couldn't imagine anyone smarter than Pa.

"You're woods-smart, Pa," she said.

Pa laughed.

"Why, I guess that's true," he said. "But I want you to be book-smart, too." He thought a minute.

"You can ride Bess to school and back," he

said. "Will that make you feel any better about it?"

It did, a little. Bess was Pa's black mare and Ruby loved riding her, but still she was scared. She dreaded going into town, where all those strangers could stare at her.

"I'm not like those town folks," Ruby said. "They'll make fun of me."

"I don't think they will," Pa said, "but if they do, you pay 'em no mind. You're just as good as they are. No better, but no worse, either."

Ma packed her a lunch pail with thick slices of bread and butter and a piece of gooseberry pie, and Ruby rode Bess down to the one-room schoolhouse where Miss Farnham taught arithmetic, history, writing, and reading.

3

WHEN RUBY ARRIVED home that evening, it was as if she'd been gone for weeks. The children shrieked and danced around Bess and pummeled Ruby with questions.

"What's school like?" Lillian asked.

"Was the teacher mean?" Marvin asked.

"Were you scared?" asked Irene.

"How tall is a giraffe?" asked Mabel, and Albert looked in Ruby's lunch pail.

"Did you eat all the pie?" he asked.

"I know," said Ruby. "We'll play school. I'll be the teacher. I'll take this big stump for my desk, and you can pick out smaller stumps for your desks. First I'll take attendance. Tell me your names." The children stared at her.

"You forgot our names?" Marvin asked.

June's eyes welled up with tears.

"Ruby fordot us," she said, sniffling. Ruby hugged her.

"No, I didn't forget you, June," she said. "See, we're playing school, and I'm the teacher, and you have to call me Miss Sawyer."

"But your name is Ruby," June said.

"Is it time for lunch?" Marvin said. "Maybe Ma would give us some pie, too."

"No," Ruby said. "We haven't even started yet. And you're not supposed to talk unless you raise your hand."

"I have to go to the outhouse," Albert said, jumping off his stump.

"Wait!" Ruby said. "You have to raise your hand before you go to the bathroom."

"It's not a bathroom," Lillian said. "It's just an old outhouse."

"You still have to raise your hand," Ruby said.

"I thought you said we had to raise our hand to talk," Marvin said.

"You do," Ruby said. "You have to raise your hand for both things."

"If you raise your hand, how does the teacher know which thing you want to do?" Marvin asked.

"Wead us a story!" June cried.

"I don't know how to read yet," Ruby said. "But as soon as I do, I'll teach you."

"Ruby!" Albert cried, wiggling.

"Okay," Ruby said. "You may go to the bathroom, Albert."

"It's too late," Albert said sadly, and stared at the puddle forming around his feet.

4

RUBY KEPT HER PROMISE, teaching her brothers and sisters words as soon as she learned them. Some nights they were still playing school when Pa came home. Ruby noticed that he listened, too, when she taught the children their ABCs and how to write their names.

Ruby had never known anything so wonderful as being able to read. She brought home stories of George Washington and Abraham Lincoln, Lewis and Clark, and Custer's Last Stand. What Ruby didn't know was that while she was at school, the other children acted out the stories she told them.

When Ma wanted to know who'd dented up her metal washtub, Marvin explained that they'd needed a boat to play Washington Crossing the Delaware, and the washtub had gotten banged up on some rocks in the river. Ruby came home one afternoon to find June and Lewis tied up in the chicken coop, crying.

"They're slaves," Irene said.

"How could you just leave them in there?" Ruby said.

"We were playing Lincoln, and I was going to free them, but I forgot," Irene said.

"Lincoln never tied up any slaves," Ruby said.

"Well, I had to tie them up before I could free them," Irene said.

Lewis's face looked swollen.

"Lewis, did you put something up your nose?" Ruby asked.

Lewis sniffled and nodded.

"What was it?"

"A bean."

"You stuck a bean up your nose?"

Lewis nodded again.

"Why?"

"'Cause Lillian told me not to," Lewis said.

Ruby tipped Lewis's head back and peered up his nose.

"There's a pussywillow up there, too!" she exclaimed.

"Don't blame me," Lillian said. "I told him not to stick that up there, either."

They all heard a shriek, and Marvin and Albert tore around the side of camp. Blood ran down Albert's forehead and continued in two rivulets on either side of his nose.

"What happened?" Ruby asked.

"We were playing Custer's Last Stand," Marvin said. "I had to whack him with my hatchet." He saw Ruby's horrified expression.

"It wasn't a real hatchet," Marvin explained. "It was just a piece of metal I found in the woods."

Ruby dipped a bucket of water from the brook to wash Albert's head.

"You look like an Indian with war paint on," she said.

"Really?" Albert said. "Leave the blood on, then."

Ruby made Albert sit with a rag held to his head and tried to call her school to order.

"Now, class, who remembers what six minus three is?"

They all looked at her blankly.

"We just went over this yesterday," Ruby said crossly. "Now, if Irene has six pieces of candy, and Albert takes three pieces, what do you have?"

"Albert's gonna have a bloody nose, too, if he tries to take my candy," Irene said.

June began to cry.

"I don't have no tandy," she said.

"It's not real candy," Ruby said. "It's pretend."

"I want some patend tandy," June sobbed, and Lewis started crying that he wanted some patend tandy, too.

Ruby closed her eyes and sighed. She'd never be a teacher at this rate.

"Class dismissed," she said. She ran through

the woods until she heard the sound of Pa's ax. She found him limbing a huge pine. He straightened when he saw her and wiped the sweat from his forehead.

"Hello there, my little jewel," he said. "What brings you out here?"

Ruby ran to him, wrapped her arms around his waist, and buried her face in his shirt. Pa always smelled of the woods, pine and spruce and cedar.

"Oh, Pa," she wailed. "I'll never be any good at teaching school."

"Ruby, I happen to know for a fact that you're going to be a wonderful teacher," he said.

"How do you know?" Ruby asked, and Pa led her to a spot where he'd swept the ground clear of old leaves. With a stick, he'd printed out his name, Ransom Sawyer, in the dirt.

"Because you already are," he said.

RANSOM SAWYER

5

JUST BEFORE CHRISTMAS, Ma had the twins, Wilson and Ben.

They were so tiny, Pa could hold them both in one hand, but they were healthy, and hungry all the time, it seemed. To help Ma get some sleep, Pa walked with them at night, and Ruby fell asleep listening to him sing the same lullabies he'd sung for her.

Pa shook her awake one morning.

"I've got a surprise for your ma," he whispered. "It's coming in on the train. Want to go with me to pick it up?"

All the way into town, Ruby wondered what Pa had ordered for Ma, but Pa wouldn't tell her.

The box was waiting for them at the station. It was the biggest box Ruby had ever seen. She traced the letters on the side of the box: P I A N O.

"A piano, Pa? You bought Ma a piano?"

Ruby couldn't wait to see Ma's face. She drummed her feet on the floorboards all the way home, trying to hurry the pung.

Ma sat down in a chair when she saw it, and tears filled her eyes.

"Oh, Ransom," she said. "How did you ever manage it?"

"I've been saving up ten years to buy you that piano, Mary," Pa said.

"It's too much," Ma said.

"'Tisn't neither," Pa said. "You deserve the finest things in life. You were a town girl before we met, and I know you gave up a lot to follow me to this camp in the woods."

"I haven't a single regret," Ma said softly. "But, oh, I have missed playing the piano."

On cold winter nights, after Pa had come home from the woods and had supper, Ma sat at the piano and sang. Ma said it was her favorite time of the day, the dishes done, and the children tired out from wrestling and exploring all day.

Pa cuddled as many children as his lap would hold, and his eyes shone as he watched Ma play.

"I feel like the richest man in the country," he said.

With her home in the woods, and school, and the stories in Miss Farnham's books, Ruby felt rich, too.

"I'd like to play the piano, too," Ruby said.

Ma promised to teach her, and she would have, too, if one of the lumberjacks hadn't walked into the camp clearing one spring day, carrying Pa's spiked boots. Ruby knew even before he'd said a word that Pa had drowned in a logjam.

6

RUBY WOULDN'T HAVE thought it possible to ever be lonely with ten brothers and sisters, but it was so lonesome without Pa she felt she couldn't breathe. She missed the smell of spruce gum on his clothes, his laugh that rattled doors, and his voice that mimicked birds and called her his little jewel.

Marvin stopped talking, and Albert started wetting the bed. June cried herself to sleep every night, and Mabel began walking in her sleep. Ma found her once on the other side of the river and never did figure out how she'd gotten there without drowning herself.

Ruby knew Ma needed her help more than

ever, knew she should be comforting the children, but she didn't have the strength. Even eating or dressing seemed to take too much effort. She couldn't bear to be in camp, for the memories of Pa pressed in on her, but when she went back to school, she found she couldn't bear to be away from camp either, for it was the only place where she could still feel Pa's spirit watching over her.

Gone were the days of carrying Pa's dinner to him and watching him work. No more nights of snuggling on his lap and listening to Ma play. Gone, too, was the home Ruby had lived in all her life, for with Pa dead, the owner of the lumber camp hired a new man to take his place cutting timber and told Ma they had to leave.

Ma sold the horses and bought a place close to town. When the other lumberjacks heard they were leaving, they took up a collection, and Jim Reilly showed up at the door with twenty-five dollars in an old metal pot.

"Mrs. Sawyer, it'd be my pleasure if you let me carry you and your belongings into town

with my team and wagon," he said.

"Thank you, Jim," Ma said. "I was wondering how I was going to get moved without the horses." Jim nodded and stared down at the ground, twisting his wool cap in his hands. When he looked up, Ruby was astonished to see tears in his eyes.

"'Twas me your husband saved the day he got killed," he said. "That jam was towering over our heads, logs all a-which-way. We got it started breaking apart, but then I got my foot caught between two logs and couldn't pull loose. Ransom saw the fix I was in and come running. He jumped on the end of one of them logs, driving the other end up, so's I could pull my leg out of there. I run for the riverbank, Ransom right behind me, but them logs toppled down right on him."

Ruby had always liked Jim; he told good stories and sometimes he brought sacks of candy from town for all of them. But at that moment, she wished it had been Jim instead of Pa that had gotten killed in the logjam.

"Mrs. Sawyer," Jim said, "I wish't it was me that'd gotten killed instead. I don't have me a family yet, and Ransom was the best riverman I ever met. He'd still be alive if he hadn't saved my life." Tears were trickling down his cheeks, and Ruby was ashamed she'd wished him dead.

They loaded their few belongings into Jim's wagon and crowded on top. Ruby felt as empty as an old sack. As she rode away from everything she'd ever known and loved, she held on tightly to Pa's wool cap and even tighter to her memories of Pa and the lumber camp. The last thing she'd done before leaving was to hang Pa's spiked boots in a tree by the river.

7

A S THEY NEARED TOWN, they passed a large white house. None of the other children took notice, but Lillian stared hard as they went by.

"Can you imagine living in such a grand house?" she said, her voice almost a whisper. "There's probably running water, and enough rooms and beds for all of us. Why, I bet there's even a bathtub!"

Ruby had passed that very house every day on her way to school, and she *had* imagined living there. She had imagined having a room of her very own and bookshelves full of books, but the wistful look on Lillian's face suddenly seemed a criticism of Pa. You didn't need money, or a big house, to be happy. The lumber camp and Pa had proven that.

The new house was just a shed, really, and when they were all inside there wasn't room to turn around, but Ma swept out the dirt and cobwebs and hung red-checked curtains on the windows.

Everyone pitched in. The boys dug up space for a garden, and the girls helped Ma plant seeds. Marvin found work at the blacksmith shop, and Albert got a job sweeping out the store.

Ma took in laundry from folks in town. Ma said with eleven children she was always washing clothes anyway so she might as well get paid for it, but Ruby hated to see Ma bent over the washtub, her red, swollen hands scrubbing clothes all day long. She hated even more hauling the pails and pails of water Ma needed for washing and rinsing the mountains of clothes.

As far as Ruby could see, the only good thing

about moving close to town was being closer to school. They lived near enough now that Lillian, Marvin, Irene, Mabel, and Albert could go to school, too. The Sawyers alone doubled the size of the school, and Miss Farnham looked startled the first morning they all trooped in together, but she was pleased to see how much Ruby had taught them. Even Albert knew his times tables up to the fives.

Miss Farnham called on Marvin to recite. Marvin rocked back and forth in his seat and wouldn't look at her.

She's gonna think Marvin's not right in the head, Ruby thought, and raised her hand.

"Miss Farnham, Marvin hasn't talked since Pa died." The other children who weren't Sawyers stared at Marvin. Marvin's face turned red, and he rocked faster. Ruby wondered if Miss Farnham would punish Marvin by making him stand in the corner, but Miss Farnham just studied him for a moment.

"I suspect he'll start talking again when he's ready" was all she said, and she let Marvin show

his work on paper. He amazed her by listing all the presidents in order.

"It pleases me to have so many good scholars," she said. "You've done a fine job teaching them, Ruby." Ruby's heart twisted when she remembered Pa telling her she'd be a wonderful teacher.

I'll study hard, she promised herself, and I will be as good a teacher as Miss Farnham.

8

J IM KNOCKED ON the door one evening with a job offer for Ma.

"Boss hired a cook from up Canada way, but he sits around drinking lemon extract till he's too drunk to cook. One day he got into the wrong barrel and put axle grease in our biscuits instead of lard! Us boys sent him packing and told the boss to hire you. Ransom always said you were a good cook."

Ruby wanted to hug him. Now they'd be able to move back to the logging camp.

"I'll take the job, Jim," Ma said. "It does seem heaven-sent, but with so many of the children in school, it makes sense for us to keep living here and for me to walk to work."

Ruby's jaw dropped.

"You see it makes sense, don't you, Ruby?" Ma said. Ruby did, but she ached to go home.

Ma had worse news.

"I'm sorry, Ruby," Ma said, "but I can't send you to school anymore. With me being gone all day, I'll need you home to help take care of the younger children." Ruby didn't argue because she knew Ma needed her, though it broke her heart to say good-bye to Miss Farnham and the wonderful books.

Ma worked hard and saved every penny she could, but, still, with eleven children, there was never enough money. One day Ma sold the piano.

"We need food on the table more than we need a piano," she explained, but to Ruby it seemed one more way Pa's memory was fading. Even Ma was forgetting him.

"Oh, Ruby, I don't need the piano to remember your pa by. My heart's just overflowing with sweet memories of him and if that's not enough, I just have to look at you. You're the spitting image of him," she said, wiping a tear from Ruby's cheek. "Except you don't have a mustache." Ma laughed.

Ma had said Ruby could read anytime she wasn't busy, but Ruby had already read all the books they owned seven times over, and besides, she was always busy. When she wasn't carrying water to wash clothes, she was weeding the garden, and when she wasn't weeding the garden, she was chasing crows out of the corn, or snapping beans, or changing the twins' diapers.

Sometimes she fell asleep at the supper table, but she tried not to complain. She knew Ma worked harder and was even more tired than she was.

In August, when the wild raspberries turned ripe, Ma handed them all empty lard pails and sent them up Butternut Hill to pick.

The other children didn't pick long before they were off chasing butterflies and looking for woodchuck holes, leaving Ruby to pick alone.

Ruby scratched at a mosquito bite. She was

hot, and tired of picking berries, too.

I wish books grew on bushes, Ruby thought, and that is when an idea came to her. Maybe there *was* a way raspberries could turn into books.

9

ON SATURDAY MORNING, in front of the store, there was a table of pies and a sign that read:

TRADE YOUR OLD BOOKS
FOR FRESH RASPBERRY PIE!

All day long, people passed by.

"Those sure look good," Mr. Skinner said. "I don't have any books, but my hound dog had puppies I'm trying to sell. I'll give you the runt of the litter."

Mr. Matheson plopped a pair of worn-out boots on the table.

"I'll take a pie," he said, and Ruby didn't have the heart to tell him her sign said *books,* not *boots.*

By afternoon Ruby had to admit her idea hadn't been so wonderful after all. She'd been up since four A.M., and all she had to show for it was a speckled pup she was sure Ma wouldn't let her keep and a pair of old boots with holes in the toes. She packed the leftover pies back into her basket to carry home. At least her brothers and sisters would be glad to help eat them.

When she passed the tall white house at the edge of town, she saw a woman seated in a chair on the front lawn. In all the times she'd walked and ridden by, Ruby had never seen anyone outside. Ruby waved, but the woman didn't wave back. Ruby was surprised. Most folks in town were friendly.

I guess living in that big fancy house, she thinks she's too good to wave to the likes of me, Ruby thought. She remembered what Pa had said, and thought, Well, I'm just as good as you are. No better, but no worse. Ruby jutted out her chin and marched past. She'd show that woman she didn't care whether she waved or not.

"Do I smell pie?" a voice said.

Ruby glanced over her shoulder. The woman had risen to her feet and was leaning on a cane. Her face *looked* friendly.

"Yes, ma'am," Ruby said. "Raspberry pie."

"Oh, I haven't had fresh raspberry pie for years," the woman said. "I can't get out to pick berries myself." Ruby realized the woman was blind. That's why she hadn't waved.

"Are you new in town?" the woman asked. "I don't recognize your voice."

"Yes, ma'am. My name's Ruby Sawyer."

"Pleased to make your acquaintance, Ruby. I'm Aurora Graham."

"I'll leave one of these pies," Ruby said. "Would you like me to take it inside for you?"

"That would be very kind of you," Mrs. Graham said. She tapped her cane from side to side in front of her as she led Ruby up the walk.

"Do you have any brothers and sisters, Ruby?"

"Yes, ma'am. Ten of them."

"Goodness!" Mrs. Graham exclaimed. "That surely is a houseful."

"Do you have any children?" Ruby asked.

"A son, Edward," Mrs. Graham said. "He lives in Boston."

The first thing Ruby noticed in Mrs. Graham's house was that every wall was covered with books.

Ruby's heart leaped. To have shelves and shelves of books to read. It was what she'd dreamed of.

"Oh," she said. "So many books!"

"Do you like to read, Ruby?"

"Oh, yes, ma'am!" Ruby said. "It's my favorite thing in the whole world."

Mrs. Graham smiled sadly.

"It was mine, too, before I became blind," she said. "What are you reading now?"

"We don't have many books at home," Ruby said. "Anyway, what with helping Ma and taking care of my brothers and sisters, I don't have much time to read." She took one last look at the books.

"I'd best be getting home," she said.

"How much do I owe you for the pie, Ruby?" Mrs. Graham asked.

"That's all right, Mrs. Graham," Ruby said. "I'd be pleased for you to have it."

10

THAT EVENING, when all the children were playing with the puppy and Ruby was telling Ma about Mrs. Graham, there was a knock at the door.

A boy from school stood holding a box.

"Mrs. Graham asked me to bring this box to Ruby," he said. "She said it was payment for a pie."

The box was full of books, books with leather covers and the titles printed in gold: *Little Women*, *Anne of Green Gables*, *Tom Sawyer*, *The Call of the Wild*, *The Secret Garden*, and *Alice's Adventures in Wonderland*.

Ruby couldn't speak. Without even seeing

her sign, Mrs. Graham had given Ruby the thing she wanted most.

"You must thank her," Ma said. She wrapped up some freshly baked muffins, and she and Ruby carried them to Mrs. Graham's house.

No sooner had Mrs. Graham opened the door than Ruby threw her arms around her.

"Thank you for the books, Mrs. Graham!" Ruby said. "It's the best gift I ever got."

"What this town needs is a library," Mrs. Graham said. "Until that happens, you're welcome to all the books in my house."

"It's really too much, Mrs. Graham," Ma said. "But I thank you, too. It's the first time I've seen Ruby smile since her pa . . . well, in a long time."

"I know how that girl feels about books," Mrs. Graham said. "I hungered after books my whole life. It's a hunger that nothing but words will satisfy. I can't read anymore, so it'd please me if my books went to someone who'd enjoy them."

That night, after she'd washed the dishes,

swept the floor, and helped put the children to bed, Ruby pulled out one of the books Mrs. Graham had given her. She carefully opened the leather cover and smoothed each page so as not to wrinkle it. She tried to concentrate on the story, but she kept thinking of Mrs. Graham alone in her house, with nothing to see but darkness, and no one to talk to.

"Ma, may I go to Mrs. Graham's and read to her?"

Ma smiled.

"I was thinking the same thing," she said.

Mrs. Graham was delighted to have Ruby's company. Ruby read three chapters of *Jane Eyre*.

"You read very well," Mrs. Graham said. "You'd make a wonderful teacher." Ruby heard Pa's voice in her head, saying the same thing, and she missed him so much her whole body ached.

"What's wrong, dear?" Mrs. Graham said.

Ruby swallowed.

"Nothing."

"I may be blind," Mrs. Graham said, "but I'm

not deaf. I can hear in your voice that something's wrong."

"I miss Pa," Ruby said. "I used to read to him, too. He couldn't read, but he wasn't dumb. He knew just about everything."

"What was your pa like?" Mrs. Graham said.

"He knew all the birds and wildflowers and trees," Ruby said. "He worked ten years to buy a piano for Ma. He said she deserved the finest things in life. At night, when we sat around listening to Ma play, Pa said he felt like the richest man in the country." Hot tears slid down the back of Ruby's throat.

"I didn't want to go to school at first," Ruby said. "I wanted to be a lumberjack like Pa."

"What made you go?" Mrs. Graham asked.

"Pa said he wanted all of his children to be smarter than he was," Ruby said.

"Goodness," Mrs. Graham said. "From what you've told me, your pa sounds like one of the smartest men I've ever heard of. There's a difference between being smart and being educated. Take my Edward. He's book-smart, but he lacks common sense."

The clock chimed twelve.

"Gracious!' Mrs. Graham said. "Is it midnight already? Time flies when you have good company. I hope you'll come back again soon, Ruby."

As Ruby walked home, her mind was full of Pa and the lumber camp. She thought of how hard she and Ma worked and how crowded they were in their little house. Yet she knew she would rather live in a shed with ten brothers and sisters and a puppy than be in a mansion alone. As poor as they were, at least they had one another.

11

MA WAS WAITING up for her.

"Mrs. Graham's so lonely," Ruby said. "Would it be all right if I invite her for supper tomorrow?"

"I think I can stretch the food to feed one more," Ma said. "She's welcome to share what we have."

Ruby stopped by the following afternoon to ask her.

"I'd be honored," Mrs. Graham said, and held Ruby's arm as they walked together.

"Please come in, Mrs. Graham," Ma said. "Children, quiet down."

"Oh, it's good to hear children's voices," Mrs.

Graham said. "My house gets so lonely."

Ma laughed.

"That would never happen here," she said. "Most times it's so noisy, I can't hear myself think." She led Mrs. Graham to the only chair in the room.

"Ruby tells me you have a son," Ma said.

Mrs. Graham sighed.

"Yes, he lives in Boston," she said. "He wants to put me in an old folks' home. I've been living alone for fifteen years, but suddenly he thinks I can't take care of myself."

"Seems to me you take care of yourself very well," Ma said.

"Thank you," said Mrs. Graham. "I wish my son saw it that way."

After supper Ma made popcorn, and they all told stories and sang songs. Ruby wished they still had the piano so Ma could play.

Mrs. Graham said she must be getting home.

"I can't remember when I've enjoyed an evening more," she said.

"Ruby will walk you home," Ma said.

The children crowded the doorway to say good-bye. When Margaret and Lewis hugged Mrs. Graham around the knees, Mrs. Graham looked like she might burst into tears. She swallowed hard.

"You're a lucky woman, Mrs. Sawyer," she said, and Ma's arm tightened around Ruby's waist.

"Yes," Ma said. "I am."

12

MRS. GRAHAM BECAME something like a grandmother to the children. If the Sawyers weren't having supper at Mrs. Graham's house, then Ruby brought her home to spend the evenings with them. Ruby could tell it did Ma good to have another woman to talk to.

Jim brought Ma home some evenings and always did a few chores before he left: cutting firewood, replacing torn shingles on the roof, fixing a cracked window.

"I don't know how I'll ever pay you," Ma said.

Jim blushed.

"No need, ma'am," he said. "It's my pleasure."

He stood by his wagon a long time without getting in.

"Is there something else, Jim?" Ma asked.

"No, ma'am, I mean, yes, ma'am, I mean, I was wondering if Miss Ruby would be willing to teach me to read."

Ruby wasn't sure she'd heard right.

"Me?" she asked.

Jim nodded.

"Your pa said he learned to read and write some just by listening to you teach the others. I reckon you can teach me, too."

Ruby could feel a smile bubbling up inside. She'd be able to be back at the lumber camp, and she'd be teaching.

"Can I, I mean, may I, Ma?" she asked, but Ma hesitated.

"I'd be happy for you to teach Jim to read," she said. "But I need you to stay with the children while I'm at work."

Jim spoke up.

"We have Sundays off, ma'am," he said. "I could come by Sunday afternoons, if it's all right with you."

Ruby was nervous that first Sunday, but Jim was so eager to learn, and so much fun, that she came to look forward to her Sunday lessons. Jim brought stories of the lumber camp and the other lumberjacks, and he smelled of spruce and fir, just as Pa had.

The other children squealed when they saw Jim coming, and they climbed his legs to hug him. Jim didn't seem to mind and handed out candy to them all. Marvin didn't say a word, but Ruby noticed he always sat as close to Jim as he could.

Sometimes, when she was teaching her lessons, Ruby noticed gray jays flitting from tree to tree, and she remembered what Pa had said about them. It was a comfort thinking that Pa's spirit was watching over her.

Jim slid into the family like a foot in an old shoe, but he took to writing hard. He'd look sorrowfully at his paper.

"Miss Ruby, I just can't seem to get the hang of it. My writing looks like moles tunneling all weewaw through a dirt pile. It don't make no sense. I'm sorry I'm so stupid."

Ruby hated seeing him so discouraged.

"Jim, how'd you learn to ride logs?" she asked.

Jim looked surprised.

"Why, when I was a young fella, I saw those rivermen driving logs and knew that's what I wanted to do when I grew up, so I just kept practicing."

"It's the same way with reading and writing," Ruby said. "You keep practicing, and pretty soon it'll be as easy as staying on top of a log."

Marvin helped Jim with his letters, the two of them silent as stones but comfortable with each other.

Ma smiled when she saw them working together.

"Who's helping who?" she asked.

Jim jumped to his feet, his face turning red. Ruby wondered why he always seemed so flustered around Ma.

"Mrs. Sawyer, the boys talk all the time about what a good cook you are," he said, and Ma laughed.

"Well, at least I haven't fed you axle grease yet," she said. "Has Mr. Bartlett hired a blacksmith up to camp yet?"

"No, ma'am, he's still looking. We've got five horses needing new shoes."

"I could do it," Marvin said.

Everyone turned to stare at him, but Jim didn't act the least bit excited.

"You've shod horses?" he asked, and Marvin nodded vigorously.

"I've been working at the blacksmith shop after school, and Mr. Gibson's been showing me how. He says I have a way with horses."

"Is that so?" Jim said. "Well, I'll tell Mr. Bartlett that I think we've found our man."

13

THE NEXT TIME JIM came, he was riding a pretty black mare.

"That looks like Bess!" Ma exclaimed.

"It is," Jim said proudly. "I tracked down who'd bought her and got him to sell her back to me. She's for Ruby."

"She's mine?" Ruby whispered.

"For teaching me to read," Jim said. "Miss Ruby, some of the other boys up to camp, they want to learn to read, too. They'd like to know, would you teach a school up there for them?"

Jim saw Ma's expression.

"Mrs. Sawyer, I know you'd be worried about Ruby alone with those rough men. But don't you fret none. I'll make sure she's safe."

"Thank you, Jim," Ma said, relieved. "I won't worry about her, then."

Marvin leaned against Jim, and June climbed into his lap, settling in, with her thumb in her mouth, just the way she used to curl up in Pa's lap. Ruby's heart ached. They were forgetting Pa. June was asleep when Jim finished his lesson, but she whimpered a little when Jim handed her over to Ma. Jim stammered as he said good-bye to Ma.

"That man's sweet on you," Mrs. Graham told Ma.

"What?" Ma said. "No! He just wants to learn to read."

"That's not the only thing that keeps him coming here," Mrs. Graham said.

Ruby's breath caught in her throat. Was it true?

"Pshaw!" Ma said, but she was blushing so furiously Ruby wondered if Ma was sweet on Jim, too.

The next Sunday, Ruby rode to the lumber

camp to give her first lesson. She'd been too nervous to eat breakfast, and she was sorry she'd agreed to teach the other lumberjacks. They were grown men. What if she didn't do a good job? What would they think of her?

The closer she got, the more nervous she got, and she was about to turn back for home when she heard *cla cla cla* and looked up to see a gray jay gliding over the treetops. She thought of Pa. He'd said she was a good teacher. She wanted to prove him right.

She rode into camp, and memories of Pa came flooding back, of the way he laughed and sang and called her his little jewel. Jim strode toward her, smiling, and the memory of Pa's last day loomed terrible in her mind, the day he'd drowned. Drowned because of Jim. Her hands were shaking, and Jim saw, but he misunderstood.

"Don't you worry, Miss Ruby," he whispered. "They're all as nervous as long-tailed cats in a room full of rocking chairs."

Ruby looked at the men standing in a cluster by the bunkhouse and saw it was true. They'd washed up for her, put on clean shirts, and combed their hair, but every one of their scrubbed faces looked scared. Ruby almost laughed. These men faced death and danger every day, and they were scared about reading! She took a deep breath, straightened her shoulders, and began her lesson. She was surprised at how fast the afternoon went, and the men seemed disappointed when she told them school was done for the day.

Jim helped her pack up her books for the ride home.

"I got something to show you, Miss Ruby," he said shyly. He held out his hand. In his palm lay a silver ring with a red stone, red like a ruby.

"You think your ma will like it?" Jim asked.

Ruby's heart took a tumble. It was true, then, what Mrs. Graham had said.

"You want to marry her?" Ruby managed to ask.

"If she'll have me," Jim answered. "I ain't asked her yet. I'm waiting till I can get us all a place to live, but when I do, you think she'll say yes?"

Ruby was too dazed to answer. It was one thing for Jim to make friends with the children and to buy back Bess. It was quite another to marry Ma. How could he think he could take Pa's place?

I can't let that happen, Ruby thought. I have to find a way to keep Ma from marrying him.

Plans swirled in her mind all week long, and she would have come up with more except Ma took sick.

14

AT FIRST IT DIDN'T SEEM too serious. Ma coughed a lot, but she pushed herself to do all the work she usually did. Then Ruby noticed Ma was sitting down to rest in the middle of cooking supper or mopping the floor. Ma's eyes were fever bright, and she coughed so hard her whole body shuddered. Ruby thought of all the books she'd read where the heroines died of consumption. She tried to hide her fear from her brothers and sisters. What would they do if Ma died?

Ma tried to stand up one morning and fell back on the bed.

"Ruby, you must go to the lumber camp and

tell them I can't cook today. I'll go as soon as I'm able."

Even the youngest children sensed something was wrong. Wilson and Ben sat wide eyed and quiet, and all the other children tiptoed around, whispering.

"Is Ma gonna die?" Lewis asked. They all stared at Ruby, their shocked little faces twisting her heart.

"Of course not," Ruby said. "She just needs to rest. I have to go to the lumber camp. Can you all be brave and behave yourselves until I get back?" Ten faces nodded solemnly at her.

"Good," she said. "Lillian, you're in charge while I'm gone."

She pushed Bess hard the three miles to camp, fear urging her on. Whatever else she thought of Jim, she knew he'd help Ma, but Jim wasn't at camp. All the lumberjacks were gone, out cutting for the day. She'd have to leave a note, but realized she hadn't brought any paper to write one. Jim would be the only one who could read it anyway. He must have some paper, she thought, from practicing his writing. Surely he wouldn't mind if she went through his things to find some. He'd want to know what was happening with Ma.

She lifted the door latch and winced as the hinges creaked. She glanced around quickly. There was no one in sight, but Ruby felt as though someone *was* watching her. She slipped into the bunkhouse and stood a few moments, letting her eyes adjust to the darkness, then moved down the bunks. She recognized Jim's shirt on one of the bunks and pawed through his things until she found a calendar. Jim had been writing on the back of the pages. Ruby tore off February and scribbled him a note. She set it on his bunk where he'd be sure to see it and tried to fold his clothes the way she'd found them. Something clinked onto the floor and Ruby heard it roll under the bunk. She got on her hands and knees and groped under the bed until her fingers touched something small and round and hard to the touch. She knew before she pulled it out what it was. The silver ring.

A picture formed in her mind, of Jim down on one knee, holding the ring up to Ma, and Ma laughing and crying, saying, "Yes, I'll marry you," and Marvin and Lillian and Mabel and Albert and Irene and Lewis and June all hugging Jim, crying, "Pa! Pa!," and Pa's spirit, like a gray jay, like smoke rising from a fire, floating away, and his memory fading until it was as if he had never lived.

Ruby couldn't let that happen. She wouldn't *let* Ma become Mrs. Jim Reilly. Jim wouldn't ask Ma to marry him if he didn't have a ring to give her. It all depended on the ring.

Ruby gripped the ring so hard it left an impression in her palm. She ran outside, not bothering to latch the door, and climbed on Bess, digging her heels in Bess's side. Bess galloped down the steep, twisting trail. Branches whipped Ruby's face, but she didn't feel them. The dangerous curve was ahead, the edge of the cliff where the land fell away and you could see the river, slicing through the valley, hundreds of feet below. Bess skidded around the corner, sending a shower of stones over the edge. Ruby lifted her arm, drew it back, and threw the ring as far as she could, down the mountainside where no one would ever find it.

By the time she got home, she wasn't shaking one bit.

15

IT WAS ALMOST DARK when Jim clattered into the yard with the doctor and Mrs. Graham sitting beside him on the wagon seat.

"Pneumonia," the doctor announced after listening to Ma's lungs. "She needs complete rest for several weeks. I don't want her lifting a finger to do anything, you understand?"

"We'll see to it," Mrs. Graham said. "Jim, how soon can you get all their things loaded and moved to my house?" Jim stared at her, then looked at Ma, and back to Mrs. Graham.

"What are you saying?" Ma said. "I'll soon be well. That'd be silly to move all our belongings over to your house for a few weeks."

"I don't mean for a few weeks," Mrs. Graham said. "I mean for good."

Even Ma was at a loss for words.

"I should have thought of it sooner," Mrs. Graham said. "You need a bigger house and I need someone to stay with me. It seems the perfect answer."

"But, how's a bli . . . I mean, a person with your condition, going to take care of . . . It'll be too much for you," Ma said.

Mrs. Graham put her hands on her hips.

"I'll have you know I was a nurse before I lost my sight. I worked in a hospital during the Civil War, caring for wounded Union soldiers. I even stood up to General Sherman once, when we weren't getting enough supplies. I guess that's why Edward hasn't managed to get me pushed into that old folks' home yet. But he'll keep trying. This way, he can't say I'm alone anymore."

"But eleven children!" Ma protested.

Mrs. Graham waved Ma's fears aside.

"They'll bring life into that stuffy old house,"

she said. "I'll help take care of them."

Jim carried Ma into Mrs. Graham's house, and Mrs. Graham settled her into one of the downstairs bedrooms. Ruby held Wilson and Ben, and the rest of the children went with Jim to gather their belongings. Mrs. Graham fixed Ma some tea and sat on the edge of the bed while Ma drank it.

"Why didn't you send one of the children over to tell me you were sick?" Mrs. Graham said.

"You didn't need to be bothered with our troubles," Ma said.

"I thought we were better friends than that," Mrs. Graham said, and Ruby heard the hurt in her voice. So did Ma.

"I'm sorry, Aurora," Ma said. "You're right. I should have told you. Since Ransom died, I've worked so hard to hold this family together, I forgot I have people I can lean on. That's what friends are for."

16

J IM STOPPED BY almost every evening with wildflowers he'd picked for Ma. He wouldn't go in her room, just stood in the doorway.

"Mrs. Sawyer," he said, "the boys all miss your cooking. Zeb Waters is filling in for you, and he's likely to poison us before you get back." Ma laughed. Ruby'd noticed that Ma always seemed to perk up when Jim was there.

"Well, with Mrs. Graham and Ruby taking such good care of me, I should be up and around in no time," Ma said.

Ruby loved Mrs. Graham's house. She had a room to herself, one of the upstairs bedrooms that looked out over the river, and even though she was too busy to read, she knew those shelves of books were there, waiting for her.

The puppy that Mr. Skinner had given her had grown into a tall, gangly hound with huge feet. He seemed to be all tongue and tail, and he knocked off three of Mrs. Graham's glass figurines before she wrapped them in newspapers and had Marvin carry them to the attic.

"I should have put them away a long time ago," Mrs. Graham said merrily. "They collect dust, and I can't see them anyway!"

Albert brought home frogs and garter snakes and baby mice that got loose in the house. After Mrs. Graham found a dead salamander in her underclothes drawer, everyone took to shaking out their clothes before putting them on.

Ruby was sweeping the floor one morning when she heard Lillian scream. She turned to see Albert dragging an animal into the house. At first Ruby thought it was a black cat, but then she saw the white stripe down its back.

Albert had a rope around its neck and he was dragging it toward Ma's bedroom. The skunk had its front legs braced, and its toenails were leaving scratches in the bare wood floor.

"Ma, look what I caught!" Albert squealed. "I lassoed him!"

"No, Albert! Stop!" Ruby shouted.

Albert turned, a hurt look on his face, and Ma sat up in bed when she saw what he had.

"Get that out of here!" she screeched, just as the skunk lifted its tail and sprayed.

17

THE BED HAD TO BE thrown out. The rugs, too. Ruby burned Albert's clothes and Ma's nightgown. Everyone else's clothes she washed in vinegar. She mopped the floor and washed down the walls and furniture, but the smell was still so strong it made their eyes water.

Ma must have apologized to Mrs. Graham about a hundred times.

"I think it's time we moved back into our place," Ma said. "Living with the Sawyer family is more than you bargained for." But Mrs. Graham just laughed.

"Oh, Mary," she said, "my life before was so

boring! Those children make me feel young again."

Jim laughed, too, when he stopped by and heard the story, but he was somber when he caught Ruby alone outside.

"Miss Ruby, you know that ring I showed you? You didn't happen to see it anywhere, did you, you know, when you left that note on my bunk?"

Ruby's heart pounded. She shook her head, afraid that if she spoke her voice would betray her.

"I can't find it anywhere," Jim said. "I don't know how I could have lost it."

"Maybe it's for the best," Ruby said, her words tumbling out. "Ma loved my pa. Just the other day she said she could never love anyone else." Ruby was amazed at how smoothly the lies slid out of her mouth.

Jim stood stock-still, his eyes darkening with pain.

"That makes sense," he said finally. "I know I can't replace your pa. Nobody could. Ransom

Sawyer was one of a kind."

A week went by, and Jim didn't show up at all.

"I hope he's all right," Ma worried. "It's not like him."

"I forgot to tell you," Ruby said, her heart pounding. "Jim said he didn't think he'd be stopping by anymore."

Ma got very still.

"Oh," she said in a small voice. She closed her eyes.

"Will you shut the door when you leave?" she asked. "I'm going to take a nap."

Ma didn't eat the soup Mrs. Graham took in to her, and she said she was too tired to join the family for supper.

"Maybe I should call the doctor," Mrs. Graham said. "She seems to have taken a turn for the worse."

Ruby knew the doctor couldn't fix a broken heart. She hadn't wanted to hurt Ma, but she'd done it for Pa. She was sure he wouldn't have wanted Ma to forget him and marry Jim, either.

Guilt made her cross with the other children, too. She scolded Irene for tearing her dress, and when Albert trailed mud into the house, wanting to show off the frog he'd caught, Ruby slapped him. He didn't say anything, just stood there. The other children stared at her, too stunned to speak. Ruby had been cross with them before, lots of times, but had never hit any of them.

"You're nothing but trouble, all of you," Ruby said, clenching her fists. "Why can't you just be good for once?"

"We'll be good, Ruby," June said, tears making her eyes look even bigger and bluer, and Lewis nodded.

"We promise," he said. "We won't be bad no more."

18

THE CHILDREN DID TRY hard to be good, and brought Ruby gifts from the woods: wildflowers, a white stone, a blue-jay feather.

"Look what I found!" Irene said, holding up a ring. "Isn't it pretty?"

The blood pounded in Ruby's head. It wasn't possible.

"Where'd you find it?" she said, more harshly than she meant to. Irene stopped smiling.

"I didn't steal it, Ruby, honest," she said. "A bird had it in his mouth. He dropped it, and I picked it up."

"A bird?" Ruby asked, and Irene nodded.

"That bird there," she said, pointing to a large gray bird perched on a branch not twenty feet away. Ruby felt her heart beating, like bird wings, against her rib cage. You never saw gray jays in town. They were birds of lonely spaces, creatures of the north woods, Pa had said. Like him. The souls of dead lumberjacks, others had said.

Ruby felt the hairs on her neck stand up. She took a step toward the bird.

"Pa?" she whispered.

The jay lifted from the branch and skimmed the tops of the trees, heading in the direction of the river. Inside Ruby's fist, the ring burned like fire.

Jim was startled to see Ruby ride into camp.

"Miss Ruby!" he said. "Nothing's happened to your ma, has it?"

Ruby shook her head. She held out her hand, but she couldn't look at him.

"Here's your ring, Jim. I lied. Ma didn't say that about never loving anyone else. I just didn't want you marrying her."

She expected Jim to get angry, to yell at her. Didn't she deserve it? She'd been horrible to him.

"I know I ain't much, Miss Ruby, and your ma ought to have better, but I love her, and I love you kids, and I want to make things easier for all of you. Your ma shouldn't have to work so hard."

Ruby felt tears tickling the corners of her eyes.

"I didn't mean to upset you, Miss Ruby," Jim said.

"You didn't," Ruby said. "It's just that you're a lot like my pa."

Jim looked like he'd been hit in the head with a peavey. He blinked a few times. When he spoke, his voice was husky.

"Miss Ruby, that there's the best thing anybody ever said to me."

19

JIM AND MA WERE married on a warm spring day when the lilacs were in bloom. For a wedding present, Mrs. Graham gave them her house.

"You can't do that!" Ma gasped.

"I most certainly can," Mrs. Graham said. "I've already put it in your name, my dear."

"What about Edward?" Ma asked, and Mrs. Graham waved her hand.

"Edward's never going to move back here. He'd just sell the house. I want it to belong to someone who'll appreciate it."

"But, Aurora," Ma said, "he is your son."

"I know," Mrs. Graham said. "But you're my family."

Ma gave Zeb Waters cooking lessons, to take over her job at the lumber camp, and Ruby and her brothers and sisters went back to school. In the evenings, Ma played the piano and Jim and Mrs. Graham sang, and every night there were the wonderful books to read.

Ruby made herself a promise. She would become a teacher, and someday she'd open a library so no one else would have to hunger for books as she had.

And, you know, she did just that. She taught in a one-room schoolhouse, then in a two-room schoolhouse, and finally in the large brick school they built on the edge of town. After teaching for fifty years, Ruby retired and built a little house on the hill where she'd been born. And she thought about the second part of her promise.

So, if you find yourself in that part of Vermont and see a sign that says LUMBER CAMP LIBRARY,

LUMBER
CAMP
LIBRARY

walk right in. In the corner, you'll see an old piano that the librarian will play, if you ask her. In the summer, she may offer you a piece of fresh raspberry pie, from berries she's picked that morning.

If I were you, I'd say yes, because Ruby makes pies even better now than she did more than seventy years ago.